Ladybird *classics*

THE THREE MUSKETEERS

by Alexandre Dumas

Retold by Joan Cameron
Illustrated by David Barnett
Cover illustrated by Fausto Bianchi
Woodcuts by Jonathan Mercer

A crowd had gathered outside the town's inn

D'ARTAGNAN

One morning in April, 1625, the little French town of Meung was in a state of great excitement. In those times, fighting was common in France. The King fought Richelieu, an ambitious cardinal. Noble families fought among themselves, and Spain was always ready to wage war with France. Few days passed without trouble in some town or another.

On this day, a crowd had gathered outside the town's inn. The cause of all the stir was the arrival of a young man on a very odd horse. It looked so comical that many of the townspeople wanted to laugh. Only the length of the sword at the young man's side, and the proud gleam in his eye, stopped them.

The young man was called D'Artagnan. He was on his way to Paris, where he hoped to fulfil his dearest wish – to become a King's Musketeer. His father had given him a letter to Monsieur de Tréville, an old friend who was now Captain of the Musketeers.

As he dismounted, D'Artagnan caught sight of a gentleman with a scar on his temple sitting at a window of the inn, talking to two other men. They were laughing, and D'Artagnan was sure that they were laughing at him. This was more than the impetuous young man could bear.

'Are you laughing at me?' challenged D'Artagnan, drawing his sword.

'I laugh as I please,' the man replied, turning away from the window and reappearing in the doorway.

D'Artagnan lunged at him in anger. Startled, the other man drew his sword. At the same moment, the innkeeper and several onlookers, anxious to prevent a fight, fell upon D'Artagnan. He was knocked senseless in the struggle and was carried indoors for attention.

When the innkeeper returned, the gentleman with the scar asked how, and who, the young man was.

'He will soon recover,' replied the innkeeper. 'I don't know who he is, sir, but he carries a letter to Monsieur de Tréville in Paris.'

'Indeed!' the other man said. 'I would like to know what is in that letter. Where is it now?'

'In the young man's doublet, which is in the kitchen,' replied the innkeeper. 'The young man himself,' he added slyly, 'is upstairs, having his wounds seen to by my wife.'

'Prepare my bill and saddle my horse,' said the gentleman as he rushed off to the kitchen. 'I am meeting Milady shortly, and then I must leave.'

Soon afterwards D'Artagnan, partly recovered, limped into the courtyard. The first thing he saw was the gentleman, talking to a beautiful young woman in a carriage.

'What are the Cardinal's orders?' the young woman was asking.

'You must return to England at once,' the gentleman replied. 'Keep a close watch on the Duke of Buckingham, inform the Cardinal as soon as he leaves London. I am returning to Paris.'

D'Artagnan rushed forward. 'Stand and fight, sir!' he demanded. 'Would you dare run away from me in front of a woman?'

Seeing her companion reach for his sword, Milady touched his arm. 'Remember,' she said quietly, 'delay could ruin our plans.'

'You are right,' he agreed. 'Go on your way, and I will go on mine.'

With that, the carriage moved off, the driver cracking his whip. The gentleman jumped on his horse and galloped away in the opposite direction.

'Stand and fight, sir!'

'Coward!' D'Artagnan called after him, but the gentleman had gone.

D'Artagnan was ready to leave for Paris when he discovered that his letter of introduction to Monsieur de Tréville was missing.

'My letter!' he exclaimed. 'It's gone!'

The innkeeper quickly proclaimed his innocence. 'That gentleman must have taken it, sir,' he said. 'He showed great interest in it.'

Whoever had taken it, the letter seemed to be gone for good. All D'Artagnan could do was hope that Monsieur de Tréville would see him without it.

AT MONSIEUR DE TRÉVILLE'S

Monsieur de Tréville was a close friend of King Louis XIII. In those troubled times, the ruler of France needed this brave man at his side. De Tréville led the King's Musketeers, a band of bold men dedicated to protecting their King.

De Tréville's greatest rival for the King's favour was the cunning Cardinal Richelieu, a man nearly as powerful as the King himself. The Cardinal had his own company of Guards, who were bitter enemies of the Musketeers. The two companies' heated battles often ended in death.

Monsieur de Tréville's headquarters was always full of Musketeers. When D'Artagnan arrived, he made his way through them, his heart

'They attacked us!'

beating with excitement. He was allowed in to see Monsieur de Tréville, but had to wait. The Captain was scolding three of his men.

'Athos! Porthos! Aramis! I hear you were fighting in the streets and were arrested by the Cardinal's Guards. This will not do!'

'But they attacked us!' the three protested. 'We fought back, and escaped.'

'The Cardinal didn't tell me that,' murmured Monsieur de Tréville. 'But I will not let my men risk their lives for nothing. Brave men are dear to the King, and his Musketeers are the bravest of them all. Now go, and I will see this young man.'

Eagerly, D'Artagnan introduced himself and told Monsieur de Tréville about the stolen letter. He explained that he had come to Paris to join the Musketeers.

'I am afraid that won't be possible until you've proven your worth,' said Monsieur de Tréville. 'No one becomes a Musketeer without first serving in a lesser regiment. But because I liked your father,' he went on, 'I will do my best to help you. I will send you to the Royal Academy, where you will learn horsemanship and the art of the sword. Then we will see how you get on.'

'You won't be disappointed, I promise you, sir,' said D'Artagnan, bowing. 'Thank you!'

As he rushed from the Captain's headquarters, D'Artagnan encountered, one after the other, the three Musketeers he had seen with Monsieur de Tréville. Still smarting from the scolding they had just received, they took offence easily, and D'Artagnan, excited and impatient, managed to upset each of them in turn. He found himself challenged to three duels that very afternoon – the first with Athos at noon, another with Porthos at one o'clock and a third with Aramis at two o'clock.

Dismayed, D'Artagnan said to himself, 'I can't draw back. But if I am killed, at least I shall be killed by a Musketeer!'

A SURPRISE
ENCOUNTER

D'Artagnan knew no one in Paris. He went to meet Athos alone, determined to fight well. But when Athos arrived, he brought the other two Musketeers with him. All three were astonished to see that they were to fight the same man.

'Now that you are here, gentlemen,' D'Artagnan said, 'I wish to apologise.'

At the word 'apologise' he saw contempt appear in their faces. They thought him a coward. His hot blood rose.

'You don't understand! I apologise only in case I cannot fight all three of you! Monsieur Athos has the right to kill me first. And now – *en garde*!'

With the most gallant air possible, D'Artagnan

drew his sword. Athos had just drawn his when a company of the Cardinal's Guards appeared.

'Sheathe your swords!' called Porthos and Aramis together, but it was too late.

'Fighting, Musketeers?' cried one of the Guards mockingly. 'You know that duelling is against the law. Put up your swords. I arrest you in the name of the King.'

'Never!' called the three Musketeers. 'There may be only three of us, but we will fight!'

'You are wrong – there are four of us,' said D'Artagnan quietly. 'Try me.'

'And what's your name, brave fellow?' asked Athos.

'D'Artagnan, monsieur.'

'Well then, Athos, Porthos, Aramis and D'Artagnan, forward!'

Swords clashed and men cried out as they fought fiercely. The Guards were good swordsmen, but at last they were beaten off.

'Put up your swords'

Afterwards, the four returned to Monsieur de Tréville's headquarters arm in arm. D'Artagnan's heart swelled with pride. 'I am not yet a Musketeer,' he thought, 'but at least I might be an apprentice.'

The incident caused a great fuss. Monsieur de Tréville scolded his Musketeers in public, but congratulated them in private. The King heard of it and was so impressed by D'Artagnan's bravery that he placed him as a cadet in the Guards of Monsieur d'Essart.

From then on D'Artagnan and the three Musketeers were the greatest of friends. D'Artagnan learned about life in Paris, and about the Court of King Louis XIII and the lovely Queen Anne. He was happy, and looked forward to the day when he, too, would become a Musketeer.

A DISAPPEARANCE

One day, while D'Artagnan was resting in his lodgings, his landlord, Monsieur Bonancieux, came upstairs to see him.

'I have heard you are a brave young man, D'Artagnan. I need help. Constance, my wife, has been kidnapped!'

'Kidnapped?' D'Artagnan asked in surprise.

'My wife is seamstress to the Queen,' Monsieur Bonancieux explained. 'And she is more than that. She is one of the few people the Queen can trust.'

D'Artagnan had heard a great deal about Queen Anne. Everyone knew that the King no longer loved her, and that she was lonely. The Cardinal once cared for her, but she had rejected him. Now he plotted jealously against her.

D'Artagnan jumped up

The English Duke of Buckingham, a powerful man in the government of his own country, had fallen deeply in love with her. But England and France were not on friendly terms.

Monsieur Bonancieux sighed. 'I think my wife was kidnapped to see if she would tell the Queen's secrets,' he said. 'Only the other day she told me that the Queen is frightened. She thinks the Cardinal has written to Buckingham in her name, to lure him to Paris and into a trap.'

'You think the Cardinal has taken your wife?'

'I fear so,' replied Monsieur Bonancieux. 'One of his men was seen nearby just as she was being abducted. He was a gentleman with a scar on his temple.'

D'Artagnan jumped up. 'That sounds like the man I met in Meung!' he exclaimed.

'Will you help me?' Monsieur Bonancieux begged. 'You are always with the Musketeers, who are enemies of the Cardinal. I thought you and your friends would be glad to spoil his plans and help the Queen.'

'I will do what I can,' D'Artagnan promised. 'And if the man who kidnapped your wife is the man I think he is, I will be avenged for what happened to me in Meung!'

D'Artagnan lost no time in telling Athos, Porthos and Aramis of the disappearance of Constance Bonancieux.

'This woman is in trouble because of her loyalty,' he told them. 'I am also anxious about the Queen's safety.'

'I have heard people say she loves our enemie the Spanish and the English,' said Athos.

'Spain is her native country,' D'Artagnan reminded him. 'It is only natural that she should love the Spanish. As for the English, only one Englishman is involved. Buckingham, chief minister to the King of England, admires her greatly. The Cardinal and his men seem to be using this admiration in some wicked plot against the Queen.'

There was no doubt in the minds of the four friends that their true enemy was the Cardinal. If they could spoil his plans, it would be worth risking their heads. The mysterious kidnapping of Constance Bonancieux was the key to the whole intrigue. She must be found, and they would look for her together.

The four men stretched out their hands and shouted in one voice:

'All for one and one for all!'

A SECRET MEETING

D'Artagnan's task was to keep watch on Monsieur Bonancieux's apartments from his own room on the upper floor. Monsieur Bonancieux had been arrested, and the Cardinal's Guards were now using his house as a trap. Anyone arriving there was taken away for questioning, to see what they knew of the Queen's affairs.

Late one night, D'Artagnan heard cries from downstairs. Realising it was a woman's voice, he drew his sword and rushed down to help. The woman was Constance Bonancieux herself! She had escaped and returned home, unaware that the Cardinal's men were keeping watch on the house. Now they were trying to force her to talk.

D'Artagnan's attack so surprised the Guards

He... rushed down to help

that they ran off, leaving to his safekeeping the grateful Constance Bonancieux .

'Thank you for saving me!' she cried. 'Now I must go – there is something I must do for the Queen!'

A few hours later, D'Artagnan was astonished to see her in a dark street with a Musketeer. What were they doing? D'Artagnan hurried to speak to them, and found the man was a stranger disguised in a Musketeer's uniform!

The stranger turned out to be the Duke of Buckingham, and Constance Bonancieux was taking him to a secret meeting with the Queen at the Louvre. 'Please don't give us away,' she begged D'Artagnan. 'You could ruin us all!'

D'Artagnan shook the Duke's hand. 'I will see that you reach the Louvre safely,' he promised.

At the Louvre, Madame Bonancieux led the Duke into a quiet drawing room where he could speak privately to the Queen. Buckingham had come to Paris in response to a message. On his arrival, he had learned that this message was in fact a trap, set by the Cardinal.

Although the Duke knew he was in danger, he refused to return to London without seeing the Queen. He waited, unafraid, while Constance Bonancieux brought her mistress to see him.

When the Queen arrived, her lovely face was pale with worry. She begged the Duke to return to England and made him promise not to see her secretly again – it was too dangerous.

'Come as an ambassador, with guards to defend you,' she said. 'Then you will be safe.'

'Very well,' Buckingham agreed. 'But please give me something of yours, so that I may wear it until I see you again.'

Queen Anne went into her chamber and quickly returned with a rosewood casket. 'Here,' she said, giving the casket to the Duke. 'Take this, and go, before it is too late!'

'Our plan has failed'

THE CARDINAL'S PLAN

Unknown to the Queen, Cardinal Richelieu soon learned of her meeting with Buckingham. The news was brought to him by the Comte de Rochefort, the very man who had so annoyed D'Artagnan in Meung. As an ally of the Cardinal, he had placed a spy in the Queen's household.

'The Queen and Buckingham met briefly,' he told the Cardinal. 'He has already left for England.'

'Then our plan has failed,' said the Cardinal angrily.

'The Queen gave Buckingham a gift,' Rochefort went on. 'It was a box containing twelve diamond studs, which the King had given her as a birthday gift.'

'Well, well!' said the Cardinal, smiling slyly. 'All is not lost!'

He sat down and wrote a letter. Closing it with his seal, he sent for a servant.

'Take this to London at once,' he ordered. 'Stop for no one.'

The letter said:

'Milady de Winter – Be at the first ball that Buckingham attends. He will wear on his doublet twelve diamond studs. Cut off two of these.
As soon as you have them, inform me.'

King Louis XIII was the next to know that Buckingham had called on the Queen in secret, for the Cardinal told him. The King demanded to know the reason for Buckingham's visit.

'No doubt to conspire with your enemies,' replied the Cardinal.

'He came to see the Queen!' insisted the King furiously.

'I am unwilling to think so,' said the Cardinal.

He was anxious to appear loyal to the Queen, but still wanted to fuel the King's suspicions. 'However, I have been told that she cried this morning, and has spent the day writing letters.'

'I must have those letters!' cried the King.

He immediately sent his chancellor to search the Queen's rooms, but the only letters he found were to the Queen's brother. The Queen was furious at the attack on her honour.

The King was remorseful. 'I had no cause to be angry with the Queen. I only hope she will forgive me,' he later said to the Cardinal.

'Perhaps if you did something to please her,' advised the Cardinal, 'her heart would soften towards you. Why not give a ball in her honour? You know how the Queen loves dancing, and it would be a chance for her to wear those beautiful diamonds you gave her for her birthday.'

The Queen was surprised and happy when she was told about the ball, and after some persuasion she did forgive her husband. Eagerly, she asked when the ball would be held.

'Cardinal Richelieu is arranging everything,' the King told her. But every day for more than a week, the Cardinal made some excuse for not setting the date.

On the eighth day the Cardinal received a letter from Milady de Winter in London. It read:

'I have them. Send money and I will
bring them to Paris.'

The Cardinal knew that Milady could be there in ten to twelve days. Content that his plans were going well, he spoke to the King about the ball.

'Today is the twentieth day of September,' he said. 'The ball will take place in the Hôtel de Ville on the third day of October. Do not forget, sire, to remind the Queen to wear the diamond studs!'

The Queen was delighted when Louis told her that the ball would soon take place. But her

The Queen was delighted

delight turned to shock and fear when he said, 'I wish you to appear in your most beautiful gown, wearing the diamond studs I gave you for your birthday.'

'When is the ball?' she asked weakly.

'The Cardinal has arranged it for twelve days from today,' replied the King.

Hearing the Cardinal mentioned, Queen Anne grew pale. 'Was it also his idea that I should wear the diamond studs?' she asked.

'What if it was?' demanded the King. 'Do I ask too much?'

The Queen shook her head. 'No, sire,' she said softly.

'Then you will appear as I ask?'

'Yes, sire.'

As soon as the King had gone, Queen Anne sank into a chair in despair. 'I am lost,' she murmured. 'The Cardinal must know everything. What am I to do?' And she began to weep.

'Don't cry, your Majesty.'

The Queen turned sharply, for she had thought she was alone. In the doorway stood Constance Bonancieux, who had heard every word of the King and Queen's conversation.

'Don't be afraid,' she told the Queen. 'I promise you that we will get those diamonds back in time for the ball!'

'I am on a secret mission for the Queen'

THE JOURNEY

Constance Bonancieux knew her husband would not help. The Cardinal had released him and given him money – he was now a Cardinal's man. But there was someone who could help – D'Artagnan. Knowing that he could be trusted not to betray the Queen, she told him everything that had happened.

'I will go to London at once,' he told her.

Realising there was not a moment to be lost, D'Artagnan asked Monsieur de Tréville if he could arrange a leave of absence for him. 'I must go to London,' he explained. 'I am on a secret mission for the Queen.'

Monsieur de Tréville looked at him sharply. 'Will anyone try to stop you?' he askcd.

'The Cardinal would, if he knew,' D'Artagnan admitted.

'Then you must not go alone,' said Monsieur de Tréville. 'Athos, Porthos and Aramis will go with you. Then surely one of you at least will get through to London.'

'Thank you,' said D'Artagnan gratefully.

Athos, Porthos and Aramis were as excited as D'Artagnan himself when he explained the mission.

The four adventurers left Paris at two o'clock in the morning. As long as it remained dark, they kept silent. In spite of themselves, they nervously expected ambushes on every side. As the sun rose, so did their spirits.

All went well until they arrived at Chantilly, where they stopped at an inn for breakfast. After the meal, the first sign of danger appeared. A stranger who had shared their table called on Porthos to drink the Cardinal's health. Porthos agreed, if the stranger would then drink the health of the King. The stranger shouted that he would drink to no one but the Cardinal. A bitter argument followed. Leaving Porthos to settle it, the others hurried on their way; Porthos would catch up with them later.

They had been travelling for several hours when they came upon men mending the road. As they drew near, the workmen drew out concealed muskets.

'It's an ambush!' cried D'Artagnan. 'Ride on!'

They spurred their horses forward, but Aramis was wounded in the shoulder and was able to travel only a little further. Athos and D'Artagnan had to leave him to be looked after at a village inn.

Only D'Artagnan and Athos were left now. They rode on, and at nightfall took a room at Amiens. The night passed quietly enough, but when Athos went to pay the bill in the morning, the landlord accused him of using forged money. Four armed men rushed in. They had obviously been lying in wait.

'Ride on, D'Artagnan!' shouted Athos, his sword drawn and ready for the fight.

D'Artagnan did not need to be told twice. He galloped on and at last reached Calais, the port from which ships sailed for England. He ran onto the quay. There, a travel-weary gentleman was asking a ship's captain to take him to England. The captain explained that the ship was ready, but the Cardinal had just issued an order – no ship was to leave the port without his permission.

'I already have the Cardinal's permission,' the gentleman said, showing the captain a paper. 'Will you take me?'

The captain agreed, but insisted that the pass had to be signed by the Port Governor. Hearing this, D'Artagnan hurried away and waited for the gentleman to come back with the signed pass.

'Ride on, D'Artagnan!'

D'Artagnan was determined that the pass should be his, one way or the other. Naturally, the gentleman refused to give it up, and D'Artagnan had to fight him for it. They fought fiercely for some time before the man at last gave in and handed over the precious piece of paper.

Breathing hard, D'Artagnan thrust the pass into his pocket and went to find a ship to take him to England.

THE QUEEN'S DIAMONDS

D'Artagnan boarded the ship just in time. They had scarcely left harbour when a cannon boomed out, signalling that the port was closed.

Worn out by his adventures, D'Artagnan slept while the ship sailed across the Channel. In the morning, he watched eagerly as the vessel dropped anchor in Dover. Soon he was on his way to London.

The young Frenchman knew no English, but he had the Duke of Buckingham's name on a piece of paper. Everyone in London knew of the Duke, and D'Artagnan was soon shown the way to his home.

The Duke, who remembered D'Artagnan

He gave a startled cry

from their meeting in the dark streets of Paris, saw him at once. His face became grave when D'Artagnan told him of the Queen's danger.

'We must return the diamond studs to her without delay!' he exclaimed. 'Louis must not find out that she gave them to me.' Taking a key from the chain he wore round his neck, the Duke unlocked the box in which the diamonds lay. As he lifted them out, he gave a startled cry: 'Two of them are missing!'

'Can you have lost them, my lord?' D'Artagnan asked anxiously.

'Never!' the Duke exclaimed. He showed D'Artagnan where the ribbon holding the two missing studs had been cut.

'Wait!' said the Duke suddenly. 'I remember now. I wore them only once, at a ball in London. Milady de Winter was there. She has never liked me, but that evening she was unusually friendly. I wondered why. It is she who must have taken them. She must be an agent of the Cardinal. How could I have been so foolish?'

He paced up and down, thinking hard. The King's ball was in five days' time. If Queen Anne appeared with two of the diamond studs missing, the King's anger would be terrible, and the Cardinal would have succeeded.

Buckingham stopped suddenly and turned to D'Artagnan. 'Five days!' he exclaimed. 'That's all the time we need. I know what we must do!'

Buckingham sent for his secretary and issued an immediate order. No ships were to sail for France, for he believed Milady de Winter was still in London. Such was his importance in the government that the order was carried out without question.

Next the Duke called for his jeweller and showed him the set of diamond studs. He promised to pay the man well to make two studs exactly like them. They must be finished within two days, and made so that no one could tell the new from the old. The jeweller agreed, and hurried away to start work.

'We are not yet beaten, D'Artagnan!' cried the Duke.

Two days later the new studs were ready. The Duke and D'Artagnan examined them carefully. The jeweller had done well. It was impossible to tell that they were not part of the original set. Now D'Artagnan could leave for France.

As his ship left Dover, he thought he saw Milady de Winter aboard one of the vessels that had been stranded there. But his ship passed so quickly that he caught little more than a glimpse of her.

Once across the Channel, D'Artagnan set off for Paris as quickly as he could.

THE BALL

Paris was full of talk about the ball, at which the King and Queen would lead the dancing. More than a week had been spent decorating the Hôtel de Ville with flowers and hundreds of candles.

The King arrived to the cheers of the watching crowds. Soon afterwards, the Queen entered the ballroom. The Cardinal, watching from behind a curtain, smiled in triumph. She was not wearing the diamond studs! He was quick to point this out to the King.

'Madame, why are you not wearing the diamond studs?' the King demanded.

The Queen looked round and saw the Cardinal looking slyly at her. 'Sire,' she said to her husband, 'I was afraid they would come to harm in this crowd. But I will do as you ask, and send for them.'

While the Queen waited with her ladies in a side room, the Cardinal gave the King the box containing the two studs Milady de Winter had stolen from Buckingham.

'Ask the Queen where these have come from,' he suggested.

But his triumph turned to rage when the Queen reappeared, proudly wearing all twelve diamond studs.

'What does this mean?' demanded the King, pointing to the studs the Cardinal had given him.

The Cardinal thought quickly. 'I wished her Majesty to have them as a present,' he said. 'Not daring to offer them myself, I adopted this plan.'

'I must thank you, your Eminence,' said the Queen. Her smile showed that she understood the Cardinal's plot completely. 'I am sure these

The Queen… gave him a diamond ring

two must have cost you as much as all the others cost the King.'

D'Artagnan watched the Queen's triumph over the Cardinal. Apart from the King, the Cardinal and the Queen herself, he was the only one in the crowded ballroom who knew what had taken place.

Later, the Queen sent for him. She thanked him, and gave him a diamond ring. D'Artagnan put it on and returned to the ball, feeling well contented. He was in favour with the King and Monsieur de Tréville, and he had helped his Queen when she most needed it. Above all, he had gained the friendship of three brave men, Athos, Porthos and Aramis. One day, he too would be a Musketeer, just like them.

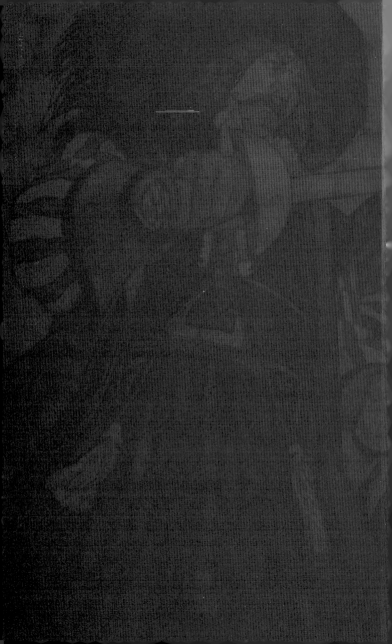